TENNIS
TRIUMPH

BY JAKE MADDOX

text by
Salima Alikhan

STONE ARCH BOOKS
a capstone imprint

Jake Maddox JV is published by Stone Arch Books, an imprint of Capstone.
1710 Roe Crest Drive
North Mankato, Minnesota 56003
www.capstonepub.com

Library of Congress Cataloging-in-Publication Data
Names: Maddox, Jake, author. | Alikhan, Salima, author.
Title: Tennis triumph / [Jake Maddox] ; text by Salima Alikhan
Description: North Mankato, Minnesota : Stone Arch Books, [2021] | Series: Jake Maddox JV girls | Audience: Ages 8–11. | Audience: Grades 4–6. |
Summary: Mira Ravi is the first-seed singles star on Hilltop Middle School's tennis team, but her life off the court is a much harder match to win as she juggles tough responsibilities at home, in school, and with her team.
Identifiers: LCCN 2020035147 (print) | LCCN 2020035148 (ebook) | ISBN 9781515882381 (hardcover) | ISBN 9781515883470 (paperback) | ISBN 9781515892342 (pdf)
Subjects: CYAC: East Indian Americans—Fiction. | Tennis—Fiction. | Poverty—Fiction. | Middle schools—Fiction. | Schools—Fiction.
Classification: LCC PZ7.M25643 Tdv 2021 (print) | LCC PZ7.M25643 (ebook) | DDC [Fic]—dc23
LC record available at https://lccn.loc.gov/2020035147
LC ebook record available at https://lccn.loc.gov/2020035148

Designer: Dina Her

Image Credits
iStockphoto: LPETTET, Cover; Shutterstock: Brocreative, design element, Denis Stankovic, (ball) design element throughout, Eky Studio, design element, Isniper, design element

TABLE OF CONTENTS

CHAPTER I

SECRETS ON THE COURT

"Go, go, go, Mira!" Coach Wallace had been watching Mira Ravi during warm-up drills lately. He wanted to make sure she didn't cut corners in her laps around the tennis court.

Mira's shoes were starting to pinch and wear. Last week, she'd tried to get away with running a bit less. But that ended up not being a very smart thing to do. She ended up having to do another lap for that. She was careful not to cut any corners today.

Mira was the first seed on Hilltop Middle School's

all-star tennis team. She knew she needed to set an example for everyone else. A lot depended on her. There were plenty of people who would have loved to be in her shoes.

If they had a clue about her life, though, they wouldn't wish that.

This was also why she didn't want to be noticed any more than she had to be. The idea of any extra attention sent chills down her back.

Mira glanced over at her best friend Addie, who was whipping along next to her doing laps. Addie played doubles for the team, and Mira played singles. Mira didn't know what she'd do without Addie. Addie was probably the kindest, funniest and most loyal person Mira had ever met.

Right then, Addie looked worried too. She always showed whatever she was feeling on her face. She didn't want others to notice Mira more than they needed to, either.

"Don't cut corners," she mouthed to Mira.

"Dynamic stretch!" Coach Wallace called, and the girls hurried to the sides of the court.

The first hour of practice was always warm-up drills and stretching. Addie made faces at Mira as they stretched, and Mira tried not to laugh. After stretches, they did footwork and reaction drills. This helped develop their reflexes. Then they moved on to actually hitting the ball.

Mira grabbed her racket and weighed it in her hand. It was too heavy. It was Addie's mom's old racket. She gave Mira all her old equipment she didn't need anymore. That meant that sometimes it didn't fit. The grip on this racket was wrong and not fitted for Mira's hand, of course. She had calluses from it already—even more than usual.

She was saving for a new racket right now. Still, it was a long way to go before she'd have enough money. Good rackets—the kind Mira wanted—could be expensive. And she really, really wanted to get one that was fitted to her hand.

She didn't mention this to Addie. If she did, Addie would tell her parents, and they did enough for Mira already. Plus, Mira wanted to do this on her own.

She tried to make her racket look light and easy in her hand so that Coach Wallace wouldn't notice anything was wrong.

Coach had them practice their forehands, and then their inside-out and inside-in backhands. He had them do volley-to-volley drills, work on their overheads, and then had them practice pivots and rotation. Finally, they did live ball match play. That was when they played someone else on the team. Mira loved playing the other girls on the team.

Mira felt the energy surging up into her arms and through her legs. Her focus narrowed completely. Soon she was only aware of the ball and her body. She loved the sharp thwack that the ball made when she hit it and when it bounced across the court.

She got paired with Kendra Malone, who was second seed on their team. Kendra was good, but

Mira was feeling *extra* good today. She got a jolt of satisfaction when her serve skimmed over the net, low and fast.

"Go, Mira!" she heard Addie shout.

She sidestepped to the middle of the court after each shot, bouncing on her toes at the baseline. Ready. Her backhands were straight down the line every time.

She wasn't even getting winded, but she managed to keep Kendra running, tiring her out. Kendra's face turned redder and redder. Usually she tried not to make Kendra mad. There were reasons you didn't want to get her mad. But today Mira couldn't seem to help it.

Toward the end, Mira showed off a little with a drop shot to catch Kendra off guard. Kendra stumbled to go after it, missing it by a mile.

Mira was still buzzing from practice as she walked back to the locker room. Soon, the adrenaline started to ebb. She realized how badly her shoes were

pinching her toes. They were really bugging her.
She bit her lip. Shoes were expensive. They were the
one thing she couldn't really buy used.

She'd have to mow so many lawns that just the
idea made her tired. Maybe if she mowed during the
day all weekend, she'd still have time to get in the
studying she needed to do at night. Keeping her
grades up was necessary if she wanted to stay on
the tennis team. She needed an A average.

Mira made sure to shower in the locker room.
At least she knew she'd get a hot shower there. When
she was done, she pulled her school uniform back on.

She always changed back into her uniform rather
than street clothes, even though the other girls usually
put on comfy loungewear after practice. Mira didn't
want the others to see her street clothes and start
wondering.

"Whose parents are driving on Thursday?"
Kendra asked loudly. She was pulling on a pair of
yoga pants. They probably cost more than all of

Mira's clothes from the last three years put together. Kendra was one of the girls who lived in a mansion in Bloomfield Hills. Her family had a housekeeper, a groundskeeper, a cook, and a nanny. Every time Kendra traveled, it was to some exotic place like Capri or Mallorca.

Before Mira started going to Hilltop Middle School, she didn't even know girls like Kendra were real. But they were everywhere here.

"Mine can't," Sienna Rigmond said, pulling on her street shoes. "Mom has a meeting and Dad's traveling."

"Mine drove last time," said Makenzie Clare. "And they're both out of town."

"Why don't *your* parents ever drive, Mira?" asked Sienna. "It's supposed to be rotating. They've never even driven once."

Mira took a deep breath. "Sorry, they can't right now . . . my mom just had surgery."

Sienna narrowed her eyes. "Two weeks ago you

said they couldn't drive because they were on some big trip. What's the deal?"

"What's your mom having surgery for?" asked Kendra.

"I'll see if my parents can drive," Addie jumped in. "I know one of them probably can. And I think Brittany said her dad can drive too." Mira looked at her gratefully. They always needed at least two big vans or SUVs to fit the team members and equipment.

The conversation eased away from who would be driving. Mira let out her breath and bent to pull on her shoes.

That was a close one.

They all filed out of the locker room. Once everyone else had left, Addie gave Mira a look that said: *It's OK, you got through that.*

"I'll text you tonight," Addie said.

They went out to the front of the school to wait with the other girls. As usual, Mira pretended someone was coming for her. But no one was.

Once everyone had been picked up, Mira grabbed her bag and walked quickly away from the school. She walked four blocks to the bus stop on the corner. She always came to this stop because she knew none of her teammates were likely to drive past here.

She put down her heavy equipment and sat down to wait for the bus that would take her all the way home.

CHAPTER 2

AT HOME

Mira took her usual seat by the window. She'd been riding the bus alone for years. Home was only about five miles away, but it felt like another world. She watched the huge, fancy school go by. Then went the wide, pretty streets of Bloomfield Hills.

The houses here were like palaces. Many of them were brick and stood way back from the road. They had huge, perfectly tended gardens and circular driveways. She loved looking at their stained glass windows and the huge maple trees in the yards. Addie said they were 1920s style houses.

Before Mira came to this school, she could hardly imagine what went on inside houses like that. Now she'd been inside some of them. She was even shocked by the kinds of after-school snacks some of these kids had. The one time she'd gone to Sienna's house with some girls from the team, her mom had served them gouda cheese on sticks, cranberries, and coconut water.

As the bus moved toward her neighborhood, the houses grew shabbier. The streets grew dirtier. They were run down, with chain-link fences, peeling paint, broken windows. There was some trash strewn around. Even the telephone poles looked crooked.

It was dark by the time the bus got to Mira's neighborhood. Once, she heard Kendra talking about how dirty the city buses are and that she wasn't allowed to ride them. As for Mira—she was so glad the bus existed.

She wouldn't have tennis if it weren't for the bus.

The bus stopped just a block from her house.

She knew none of the girls from tennis would be here.

But she looked around anyway before she jumped off the bus.

She headed for her house. Addie knew where she was from, of course, but none of the others did. She hurried down the street, the way her mom always told her to do once it got dark. In her neighborhood, the streets weren't always safe at night.

Their little house looked like it had been leaning to one side for what seemed like years. It had peeling, light blue paint. But Mira loved the special shade of blue. It wasn't quite robin's egg blue, and not quite sky blue, but something in between. She also loved that she could see the big oak tree out front from their kitchen window.

Mrs. Johnson was in her yard next door, pulling her trash out. "I hope school was good today, Mira," she said and smiled. "Sean's inside."

"Thanks." Mira smiled back and hurried to Mrs. Johnson's back door. She heard her little brother, Sean, playing a video game in the living room.

Mira came into the room and picked up his backpack. "Time to come home," she told him.

He stuck his tongue out at her and kept playing.

Their mom was always working. Sean was only seven, so he went to Mrs. Johnson's after school until Mira got home. To repay her, Mira mowed Mrs. Johnson's lawn and her mom cleaned her house on the weekends.

Mira's dad died when she was much younger. Her mom had to start taking care of her and Sean by herself. It was really hard. All their other family— aunts, uncles, and cousins—were back in Hyderabad, India. She'd never even met them.

For a while, her mom worked as a housekeeper at a hotel. But when the hotel closed, she had to get two jobs just to make enough money. She worked at another hotel and at a restaurant bussing tables. That was why she was always gone these days.

It also meant Mira was stuck with Sean most nights.

Mira could tell it made her mom sad. She wished she were home with them. She always told Mira that she was a good sister and a big girl. Still, sometimes Mira just wanted to crumble. Sometimes she just wanted to come home and flop onto her bed and think her own thoughts, do her homework, eat dinner, and go to bed, like Addie got to do. Like all her classmates got to do.

She didn't tell her mom that part, though.

Sean put down his video game controller with a loud sigh. Then he followed Mira back to their house.

"Did you do your homework?" Mira asked him.

Sean flopped down in front of their TV and turned it on. "No."

She turned off the TV. "Then you have to do it soon."

"You're not the boss of me!" he shouted.

She rolled her eyes. "You'll do what I tell you. If Mom's not here, I am the boss of you. Go wash up for dinner."

He stuck his tongue out again and headed for the bathroom.

She opened the fridge and exhaled. It was empty, except for half a carton of milk. Her mom hadn't shopped today. She probably wouldn't get paid until tomorrow. That meant nothing for dinner and probably nothing for breakfast.

Hopefully her mom would get the stuff to make keema samosas and biryani rice. Those were Mira's favorite Indian dishes. Her mom always said the Hyderabadi versions were the best of both. Mira's mouth watered at the thought.

For now, though, thank goodness for the Hilltop cafeteria. Mira opened her backpack and pulled out the food she'd managed to sneak out of school that day. She'd gotten two turkey sandwiches, an apple, an orange, a few mini boxes of cereal, two bags of chips, a bag of pretzels, and two cookies.

She put the cereal and fruit away for the morning. She dumped the rest of the food onto plates and called Sean to the table. Sean grumbled that there was no cheese on his sandwich. He ate the whole thing anyway. Afterward, Mira cleared the table.

"Homework time," she said. She already felt exhausted.

Sean grumbled again, but he got out his reading book. He frowned at it. "What's this word?" he asked, pointing.

She squinted. "Hea-vi-ness. Let's sound it out together."

"I hate homework," he said.

"I know," she said. "But we have to do it."

She glanced at the clock. She hadn't even started her homework yet. And she had a mountain of it.

Sean bounced up and down in his seat. He couldn't sit still. He finished his reading homework. But if she didn't do something to wear him out, he'd never go to sleep.

"Tennis?" she asked him.

"Yeah!" he cried.

21

She grabbed the old, beat-up racket she'd bought for him at a garage sale, and took him out back. The moon was bright enough to light up the back of the house, part of which was concrete. Their mom hated when they practiced against the house, but they did it all the time when she wasn't home. It was especially fun at night, when the moon shone down on the house.

"OK, forehand drills," Mira said. "Only forehand—can't use your backhand at all for these. Go!"

Sean didn't have a bad forehand for a seven-year-old. Right now, she was working on his stance. She was trying to teach him to keep a big enough space between the racket and the side of his body to make sure his grip was correct.

He giggled as he bounced on his toes, slamming the ball as hard as he could. He missed half the time, scrambling after the ball in the dark. When he was done, he was panting and sweating.

"OK, that's enough. Bedtime," she said.

He was so tired he got right into bed. Then he made Mira stay with him while he told her about the nightmares he'd been having. By the time he fell asleep and she tiptoed out of his room, it was 10 p.m.

She hadn't even started her homework yet.

CHAPTER 3

STAYING AWAKE

Mira was so tired she wanted to fall over. She'd hoped to stretch some, but homework was more important. She had to read two chapters for social studies and finish a math practice set.

Hilltop was no joke. The teachers assigned a ton of homework. Her mom, of course, thought this was a good thing. She said it meant Mira would get to go to college and wouldn't have to struggle like she did.

Mira went to her room and flopped onto her bed. She forced herself to keep her eyes open and pulled out her books. She also pulled out the one treasure she had, the phone that Addie had given her for her birthday. Before that, she didn't have a cell phone at all. Her mom wasn't sure about it at first. Now, though, her Mom liked it. It meant she could text Mira easily.

There was a text from Addie: *Close call today.*

Mira answered: *Yeah. I watched Sean tonight. I'm only just starting homework. Thanks for covering for me!*

Addie: *You're welcome. The social studies chapters are hard.*

Mira: *I know. I hope I stay awake.*

The Meyers had done so much for her. Mira had only met them this past summer, but she felt like she'd known them forever.

Before last summer, she used to take the bus across town to the big, spotless Hilltop Middle School tennis courts whenever she could. She loved to practice her serve whenever other kids weren't there. She'd pretended she was on their all-star tennis team.

She'd always been fascinated by tennis, ever since

she saw it on TV when she was little. Two years ago, her mom found her an old racket at the thrift store. Mira had started practicing on her own every day.

Last summer when she was at the courts, Addie's family had shown up to practice. They watched Mira for a while before she realized they were there. Then Addie had asked if Mira wanted to play. It was so much fun.

Afterward, Addie's parents asked Mira all kinds of questions. They wanted to know where she went to school. They asked if she was on a tennis team or had a coach. She explained that she lived across town and came here to play. They said she should apply to Hilltop. Then she could be on the tennis team with Addie.

Mira couldn't believe it. She was so excited, until she did a little bit of research. She realized that she didn't live in Hilltop Middle School's district. And out-of-district kids had to pay thousands of dollars per year to go there.

Her mom looked sadder than ever when she heard that. "Sorry, baby," she said in Hindi. "You know there's no way."

But Addie's parents told Mira she should apply anyway. They offered to let her use their address on her application. It was the nicest thing anyone had ever done for her. So she told the school she lived at Addie's house. That was how Mira could go to Hilltop and play on the team.

But that was also why no one could know where she really lived. They'd kick her out once they realized she lived out of district. She couldn't pay the out-of-district fees. Her mom felt bad about being dishonest. Still, she wanted Mira to stay at Hilltop. It meant that she could get into a better high school and college. Mira wanted that too. Mostly she wanted to keep playing tennis, no matter what. She loved it so much that it was practically all she thought about.

Before Mira turned to her homework, she got out her laptop. She couldn't believe she had one now.

The school loaned them out to all the students.
She carried her laptop around the house until she managed to get on Mrs. Johnson's Wi-Fi. Her mom didn't pay the bill last month, so they didn't have their own Wi-Fi right now.

Once she was online, Mira browsed for a new racket. Well, new for her—she scrolled used rackets people were selling. She looked at some new ones, too, and almost drooled. She couldn't believe how much brand new rackets cost.

She didn't find one that she could afford. She sighed. She'd need to find one soon. Her wrist and hand were starting to hurt because the grip was so wrong.

She finally turned to her homework. It was midnight now. She got the math done. She managed to read a chapter of the social studies before she fell asleep, right on the pages.

CHAPTER 4

NO SECOND CHANCES

Usually, Mira liked to get to school early and hit the courts for a few minutes before class. It cleared her head and got her ready for the day. But today on the bus, she frantically tried to read the second chapter in her social studies book. She was kicking herself that she'd fallen asleep before she read it last night.

Mira tried hard to focus. Even after reading each paragraph a few times, nothing seemed to be sticking. She was so tired that the words swam together in front of her. Before she knew it, she was near school.

She always got off at the stop several blocks from school and walked the rest of the way. Addie said this was going overboard, but Mira didn't want to take any chances. The last thing she needed was Sienna or Kendra asking her why she took the city bus to school.

She was too late to get in any practice before school. That was a shame, because usually practicing by herself calmed her down. On the way to her first class, social studies, Mira passed by Coach Wallace in the hall.

He stopped her. "Mira!" he boomed in a loud, happy voice. "I'm requesting that all parents attend the match this Saturday. Your mom hasn't been to one yet, right? Let her know for me, will you?"

Mira froze. For a second no words came out, but then she managed to say, "Does she have to come?"

"Your mom is the only parent I haven't met," he said.

She forced herself to nod. "I'll ask her. She might be working that day, but I'll ask."

She smiled one more time and ducked away down the hall. Her heart pounded so hard she wanted to throw up.

Her mom hadn't been able to come to any matches yet. Secretly, Mira was a little relieved. She worried that her mom or Sean would say something that would give away where they lived. Her mom's English wasn't very good. She might easily get things mixed up. And then Kendra and Sienna might wonder how they could afford out-of-district tuition. It wasn't worth the risk.

But what if Coach Wallace called her mom and asked her to come? The school had her mom's cell phone number, but Addie's parents' address. What if he realized that they didn't match up?

Mira felt sick to her stomach as she sank into her seat in social studies.

Addie sat down next to her. "What's wrong?"

"Coach wants my mom to come to the next match," she whispered.

Mr. Huron passed out the quizzes. Mira tried to focus. Some of the questions were from the first chapter she read last night. Most of them were from the second chapter she tried to read on the bus. She tried to remember the information, but it all blurred in her mind.

By the time Mira was done, her hands were so sweaty that she could barely hold the pencil.

She knew she'd failed the quiz. She'd guessed on half the questions.

She told Addie that she needed to talk to Mr. Huron. She waited until everyone else had filed out. She approached the teacher's desk. He was looking over the papers they had just handed in and didn't notice her at first.

"Mr. Huron." Mira's voice came out in a squeak, so she forced herself to start over. "Is there any way I can retake the quiz?"

He looked at Mira over his glasses. "What makes you think you'll need to retake it?"

Mira shifted on her feet. "I don't think I did very well. I . . . I couldn't remember the answers from chapter two."

Mr. Huron raised his eyebrows. "I'm sorry, but I don't allow makeups for nonemergency reasons."

Mira's chest deflated. "But I need good grades to stay on the tennis team," she whispered. "I have to keep up an A average. Even one B or C could mean getting kicked off the team."

Mr. Huron shook his head. "Mira, you're a good student. I wouldn't worry about one quiz. But you'll need to study harder."

Mira left the class as quickly as she could. She felt sick. If her social studies grade tanked, would they give her some time to improve her grade? Or would they kick her off the tennis team right away?

Maybe she could beg Coach to give her a second chance if that happened. But that would mean he'd ask why she needed a second chance. He'd want to know why she wasn't doing better in school. If she told him she was too tired or distracted, he'd probably think she was too distracted to play tennis too.

No. The only way was to make sure her grades stayed up.

She walked toward her locker. Frantically, she thought of ways to make sure she had some time for herself that night. She needed to catch up on homework. Her mom would be working late again.

She almost bumped into Kendra and Sienna.

"Watch yourself, girl," Kendra said, laughing. "Look where you're going."

Mira smiled and pushed past her. Inside, though, she felt a fiery anger. Kendra and Sienna used to talk about how they were almost failing math. But their parents hired tutors to help them. Now they were doing better.

Mira had barely heard the word tutor until she came to this school. These tutors actually went to kids' houses and worked with them. Sometimes they spent hours working with them on just one subject. She couldn't even imagine having that kind of help. The idea of her mom being able to afford a tutor almost made her laugh.

She went to her next class, wondering if she should offer Mrs. Johnson some more lawn-mowing sessions in exchange for watching Sean that night.

CHAPTER 5

ALMOST CAUGHT

"Hi, honey," Mrs. Meyers called out, as they pulled their big SUV into Mira's driveway on Saturday morning. Addie's parents were picking her up for the tennis match at Wellington. They were the only people from Bloomfield Hills who were allowed to see her house.

Her mom was home for once. Thank goodness she could watch Sean that day. She had to go in to work at her restaurant job that night, but at least Mira would have the day free. When she got back from the match she'd have to start mowing lawns. She tried not to think about that.

Her mom came out and greeted Addie's parents. A million different emotions showed on her mom's face as she looked at their huge, shining car. Mira knew her mom was sad that she couldn't provide those kinds of things for her and Sean. Her mom was embarrassed that Mr. and Mrs. Meyers helped so much. But she told Mira she was also grateful, because she wanted her to be able to play tennis.

"Hello," her mom said. She was self-conscious about her English, but she felt comfortable with the Meyers family.

"Hi, Sabra," Mrs. Meyers said to her warmly. "How are you?"

Her mom smiled and said, "Good. How are you?"

Mira lugged her equipment out to the car. Mr. Meyers hopped out to help her.

"You excited?" he asked, lifting her racket bag into the trunk. A hand-me-down from Addie, it was really big. She could fit her racket, tennis shoes, water bottle, and wrist- and headbands inside it.

"Yeah." And she was. She was full of energy. Before a match, a weird thing happened to Mira. Every other problem in her life drained away, and she just focused on the game. It was like the sound of the rest of the world stopped. This happened even when she was extra worried and stressed, like she had been that week. And that excitement always started way before she'd even left for the match.

Addie rolled down the window and grinned. "I'm excited!" she said. "We're going to cream Wellington."

Mrs. Meyers and Mira's mom talked for a bit, and then they all loaded up. Mira slid in between Addie and her little brother, Henry, who was four. He was sitting in his car seat. He started telling her all about the new train set he got for his birthday.

As they drove away, Mira got the weird thought that always made her feel guilty. It was the thought that she belonged in this world, with Addie's family and school, rather than in her own neighborhood. But then when she was back home, she got the same feeling in reverse. Then, it was like school and Addie were a whole world away. When she was home, she felt like she belonged with her mom and Sean, in their world.

She couldn't explain it. It was weird not knowing exactly where she belonged sometimes. She tried not to think of her mom's sadness when she saw the car. Mira pushed it out of her mind and pasted a smile on her face.

Before they knew it, they were at Wellington Middle School. It had one of the best tennis teams in the area. Hilltop had been waiting all season to play them.

"I'm so excited," Addie squealed as they crossed the parking lot to the school.

While they were in the locker room getting changed, Kendra and Sienna came up to her. "Where's your mom?"

"She couldn't come," Mira said. She tried not to let them see her hands shaking as she tightened her shoelaces. "She's working today."

Kendra frowned. "I thought you lived near our school?"

Mira's throat stuck. "I do."

"Then how come your mom works so much?" Sienna said. "Do you guys live in a guesthouse on someone's property?"

Mira stared at them. They were talking about all the Bloomfield Hills houses that had guesthouses or garage apartments. Sometimes the housekeeper or groundskeeper lived there.

"No," Mira said. "We have our own house."

"Where?" said Kendra. "What street?"

"None of your business." Mira's face was flaming. She tried to push past them.

They followed. Kendra was snickering to herself. "Girl, I'm going to follow you home one day and solve this mystery once and for all."

She tried to make it sound like she was joking, but Mira knew she wasn't. Kendra would follow her home. She made it her business to know everything about everyone.

Mira was still shaking when she met the team for warm-ups. They did laps around the court. Then they ran lines back and forth and stretched.

"You OK, Mira?" Coach Wallace asked her.

"I'm fine." She focused on the ground as they gathered around him. She reached for Addie's hand for a second and squeezed it, just to know it was there.

Addie gave her a questioning look.

Mira mouthed, *I'll tell you later.*

Coach Wallace wound them up before they went out. He reminded them they were awesome and told them to focus. Mira was out first, against Krissy Albert from Wellington.

As she stood across the net from Krissy today, she felt different than she ever had before a match. There was no calm concentration. There was no focus or joy. She was just a ball of nerves, standing there terrified.

It was her serve. "Love serving love!" she shouted, which in tennis means "0 serving 0." It was the beginning of the set, and neither of them had any points yet.

She knew she was in trouble right away when she just couldn't seem to nail the serve. On her first try, she hit it into the net. On her second serve, she hit a let. That meant she'd have to serve again.

Her brow began to sweat. She could almost *feel* Coach Wallace wondering what the heck was wrong with her. At the same time, she sensed Krissy's glee that she was so off her game. On her third serve, Mira got the ball in. But it was a safe shot and there was no power behind it.

Krissy hit it back easily with a short return, sending it hard and fast across the net. Mira had to run for it. Still sweating, heart pounding, she kept going. But she was hitting the ball too far behind her.

She wasn't getting to it right off the bounce. She also played balls that were clearly headed out of bounds. Again, Mira imagined what Coach Wallace was thinking.

In the end, she lost on a foot fault. It was a rookie mistake and so embarrassing. A perfect finish to the most horrible set she'd ever played. She lost the first set 0–6.

"Mira," Coach Wallace called.

She tried to keep her head up as she walked toward him, but it wasn't easy. She tried hard to ignore the stares coming from other parts of the stands. The Wellington crowd cheered.

Coach Wallace looked worried in a way she'd never seen before. "Hey," he said. "Get some water. Hydrate. And listen up—you're hitting off your back foot. And you're losing confidence in your first serve. Get her off balance. Don't let her control the game. You're playing defense the whole time, and we need you to play offense."

She nodded numbly. His words felt like they were coming from far away.

The second set was no better. She'd lost the control she'd had at every other match she'd played. She hit everything long and wide. She double-faulted an entire game away early in the set. She couldn't get it back after that.

She lost 0–6 within twenty minutes.

Again, she blocked out the Wellington cheers as she moved to the net to shake Krissy's hand, still numb.

CHAPTER 6

CONFESSIONS

Mira walked off the court, feeling more panicked than ever. She didn't meet Coach Wallace's eye, even as he followed her out and past the stands.

"What happened out there?" She could tell he was worried, frustrated, and surprised all at once.

She couldn't look at him. She looked at the ground again. She tried to block out the whispers of other girls on her team as they stared at her. She knew they were talking about her.

Mira wondered if Kendra and Sienna had any idea that what they said upset her. She hoped not.

She walked into an alcove in the hallway of the school.

Addie rushed over. "What *happened* to you?"

Mira looked at her and tried her hardest not to cry. "I'm going to get kicked off the team."

"Why would you say that?" Addie said. "Everyone makes mistakes. It'll be OK."

"No, it won't."

Mira burst into tears. Then she told Addie everything. Addie's eyes got wider and wider. She'd known about some stuff, but not all of it. Mira finally told Addie how often she had to watch Sean. She told her that she barely had time for homework, which meant she might get kicked off the team. She told her she needed new equipment and couldn't afford it.

By the time Mira was done, Addie was almost crying too.

"Mira, I had no idea how hard it's been," she said. "We can help you buy new equipment, don't worry . . ."

Mira sniffled and wiped her face. "It won't matter

soon anyway. Not after everyone finds out where I live. I won't be in the program or at school anymore."

Addie glanced toward the door. "Do you really think Kendra and Sienna would do something?"

Mira felt in her bones that they would.

"Yeah," she said. "I'll just have to lay low for a while."

"Kendra has always wanted first seed," Addie fumed. "That's what it is."

Mira nodded. She was so tired. All the excitement she'd had just a few hours ago drained out of her. She felt like an empty balloon.

"There's one other really important thing you should do," Addie said.

"What?" Mira asked.

"Talk to your mom and my parents. You have to tell them what's really going on."

CHAPTER 7

RADICAL HONESTY

After the match, Addie's parents drove her home. Mira asked if they would wait while she ran in and asked her mom something.

"Sure," said Mrs. Meyers.

Mira rushed into the house and found her mom in the kitchen. "Mom, Mr. and Mrs. Meyers just dropped me off. They're still outside. There's some stuff I want to talk to you both about. Is it OK if they come in? I can talk to you about it in private first if you want."

Her mom looked worried. "No, it's fine. But at least let me get some coffee ready."

Mira ran back out and asked if Addie and her family could come in for a minute. They looked a little confused but turned the car off and came in.

A minute later Mira found herself sitting at their kitchen table with her mom, Addie, and Addie's parents. Sean took Henry to play video games in the living room.

"I need to talk to all of you," Mira said. She translated into Hindi for her mom.

All three parents looked concerned. Addie sat next to Mira, holding her hand.

"Mira, tell us what's going on," her mom said, worried.

"Mistakes happen in matches, if that's what this is about," Mr. Meyers said. "You tried your best, and that's what matters."

"It's a lot more than that," Addie said, squeezing Mira's hand. "Tell them."

She took a deep, shaky breath and started to talk. She told them the things she'd told Addie. As she did, her mom's eyes filled with tears, and she looked ashamed.

"I'm not blaming you, Mom," Mira said. "I'm happy to help. It's just that now . . . I need some help."

She felt embarrassed and ashamed too. She'd done well so far, acting like she didn't need much every time Addie's parents offered.

"But," Mira finished up, looking at her mom, "I don't want you to think I can't work hard and help out. I do work hard, I promise. It's just that at this rate . . . I can't do all the work I need to do to be able to stay at Hilltop."

When she was done talking, her mom hugged her. She was crying. "I'm sorry it's so hard for you," she said. "We're going to figure something out. I will see if Mrs. Johnson can take Sean for longer on the weeknights, so you can do your work."

"I'm so sorry, honey," Mrs. Meyers said. She glanced at Mira's mom. "Do you mind if we try to help too?"

Her mom shook her head. "I don't mind," she said. "Thank you."

Mira rubbed her forehead. She was exhausted and nervous. But she also felt like a brick had been lifted off her chest.

"I have an idea," Mr. Meyers said. "If your mom is OK with it, how about we hop online and look for scholarship opportunities?"

"What are scholarship opportunities?" Mira asked.

"A scholarship is when people get awarded money to be able to do something. Sometimes it's to go to a certain school or play a certain sport. If you get scholarship money, it could help with some of the challenges you're facing."

Mira pulled out her laptop, and everyone gathered around it to start helping her look for scholarships. Mr. Meyers showed her all kinds of places that were awarding scholarship funds for low-income students. Some of them were national, meaning anyone in the country could apply. Some of them were local, so only people in Detroit or Michigan were eligible. Mostly they were sports and academic scholarships.

Mira stopped scrolling and shouted, "Look at this one!"

She'd landed on one called the *Rick Morris Memorial Scholarship for Student Athletes.* Her eyes lit up as she bent toward the screen.

"Wow, that does look good," said Mr. Meyers.

"So what do I have to do?" Mira asked.

He scrolled through the site. "It says you need to fill out a few forms and write an essay. That's all they want for now. It says if they're interested, they'll ask for more information."

"What does it say?" her mom asked anxiously.

Mira translated for her mom. Then she asked, "An essay? What do I tell them?"

Mr. Meyers smiled. "They want to know about the challenges you face. Tell them the truth. Tell them everything you just told us. This is a good time to practice radical honesty."

"What's radical honesty?"

"It means being very honest without holding anything back," Mrs. Meyers said.

"But—what if they don't pick me?"

"Well, they might not," Mrs. Meyers said with a shrug. "But how will you know if you don't try? No matter what, this is good practice for putting yourself out there. And if they don't, we'll all keep helping you figure out how to make this work."

She translated for her mom, whose eyes lit up with hope. "Could this work?"

"It might," Mira told her. She felt shy all of a sudden. "OK. I'll write them an essay tonight before bed. I need to think about it."

"Fair enough," said Mr. Meyers. "And in the meantime, Sabra, do you mind if we help Mira out with some new tennis equipment? It could be an early Christmas present."

Mira translated for her mom, who blushed, smiled and nodded. "Thank you," she said.

"You guys have done so much for me—" Mira said, her face flaming.

"Addie didn't have a close friend at Hilltop until you came to school," Mrs. Meyers said. "You've given her a lot too."

"Yeah." Addie nodded. "Everything's so much better with you there."

Mr. Meyers looked right at Mira. "One day when you're a famous tennis player, you can pay it forward."

"What does that mean?"

"It means you can help someone else who needs help, the same way you do right now," he said. "There's nothing wrong with needing help. It's brave to ask for it."

Mira nodded. She looked at Mr. and Mrs. Meyers. "Thanks for everything you guys do for me. I'm going to pay you back for the racket with my lawn mowing money. I want to buy that myself." She turned to her mom and added in Hindi, "And thanks for everything, Mom."

"I'm sorry, Mira," her mom said, wiping her face. "I'm proud of you, but I wish you didn't have to do this."

"It's all right, Mom," Mira assured her. "It will be exciting to tell the story of our family and how you came here."

Her mom squeezed her hand. "You're brave. I want you to be honest in your essay. Just like you were honest with us tonight."

"Thanks, Mom," she whispered.

Mrs. Meyers said, "We're all happy to help."

* * *

Later that night, Mira's mom helped her fill out the scholarship forms before she went to bed. Mira stayed up in her room to write the essay. She thought long and hard about what she wanted to say. She tried to remember what Mr. Meyers said about "radical honesty."

She started off talking about herself and her life. But before she knew it, she was talking about what life was like for all kids like her. She explained what it was like when you wanted to do something more than anything in the world, but you have all this stress and these things holding you back. She described how different her life was from those of her teammates. She explained how tired and hopeless she felt.

When she was done, it felt like she'd gushed out a river of feelings. She couldn't believe she'd told a bunch of strangers all of that. It was stuff she never told anyone. But Mr. Meyers said it was exactly the kind of thing they needed to hear.

She took her laptop downstairs and found Mrs. Johnson's Wi-Fi. Then she sent the application before she could chicken out. She'd translate the essay for her mom in the morning. Right now, it was just for her.

CHAPTER 8

FOUND OUT

Ever since Mira sent the scholarship essay and told her mom and the Meyers family about what was happening, she felt lighter.

At practice on Thursday, Kendra did what Mira had known she would do. She walked right up, head high, and said, "I challenge you for first seed."

Mira glanced at Coach Wallace.

He nodded. "One set."

They had a match that weekend against Bremerton, and Mira had no intention of giving up first seed. She went on the offense right away. She knew Kendra's backhand wasn't strong, so she hit everything deep and hard. She moved Kendra back and forth, kept her running. She kept the balls just above the net, on point with her volleys.

Kendra was tired. Mira could tell she had been hoping Mira had lost it.

Mira drew Kendra up close and lobbed to her backhand. Kendra swung and missed.

Mira let out a breath. She'd beat Kendra 6–1.

Addie came up and clapped Mira on the back as Kendra walked away. Kendra's face was scrunched with rage. Sienna ran to catch up with her, looking just as mad.

Mira couldn't help feeling satisfied as she left the court. But she was a little nervous too. She'd never seen Kendra and Sienna so mad.

By the time she was done with her shower and back in the locker room, she was fully expecting them to rail at her.

But instead of being mad, Kendra and Sienna were actually smiling as they changed out of their clothes. Mira stopped in her tracks and stared at them. They were being weirdly quiet.

"Why's she so quiet?" Mira whispered to Addie. "She was spitting mad out on the court."

Kendra packed up and followed Sienna from the locker room. They smiled at Mira and Addie on the way out.

It gave Mira the chills.

"They're up to something," she told Addie, stuffing her racket in her bag. "I know it."

"Well, try not to think about it," Addie said nervously. "I'll text you tonight."

They headed out into the hallway. Addie went toward the front door, but Mira hung back.

"Aren't you coming?" she asked.

Mira shook her head. "You go ahead. I want to wait a while to make sure they're gone."

"All right."

She watched Addie leave. Then she followed slowly and stood by the front doors looking out. She waited a full thirty minutes. She didn't leave until the janitor told her he needed to lock up the school.

She headed to the bus stop. It was dark already. She swept her gaze down the street for Kendra, waiting for her to jump out of the bushes.

Luckily, she made it onto the bus safe and sound. She told herself to calm down. Instead, she sat there jiggling her foot and wondering what Kendra was so happy about.

She tried to push it from her mind. She thought instead about the new racket Mr. and Mrs. Meyers ordered for her. Addie had told her about it earlier.

She was still a little embarrassed about this, but she was also relieved and happy to be getting a new racket. She closed her eyes and imagined how light it would feel in her hand, and how solid the grip would feel. And she was glad she'd be paying them back with her own money.

Before she knew it, she was home. She walked quickly toward her house. Her mom was actually home tonight.

That's when she first noticed the car. It was crawling behind her, slowly. Its headlights were bright.

She started sprinting for her house, her mind wild with fear. Her mom always told her to run anytime a car was acting weird. She'd never had a car follow her like this.

She reached her front porch, breathless. She turned around. The car was slowly passing her house.

The passenger window went down.

And there were Kendra and Sienna's faces. They stared at her from the car, as she stood frozen on the porch of her house. Their eyes widened. Sienna laughed. Then the car sped up and was gone.

Mira's heart galloped around. She stared after the car. She knew Sienna had an older sister that picked her up sometimes. That must have been her sister's car.

She ran in the house, up to her room, and called Addie. Breathlessly, she told her what happened.

"Maybe she won't say anything," Addie said when she was finished. "After all, she'd have to basically admit she was following you."

"She'll definitely say something," said Mira. "She'll find some way."

"She doesn't know you're not paying the out-of-district tuition," Addie added. "For all she knows you could be."

"Maybe," Mira said, thinking of the gleeful smile on Kendra's face.

Mira's mom knocked on her door. "Mira! Come and help me with dinner, please."

* * *

The next morning before the bell rang, Kendra and Sienna came right up to Mira in the crowded school hallway.

"So why'd you lie about where you live?" Kendra's eyes narrowed. "My sister says it's probably because you're not paying tuition. You must be lying about being in district."

Mira tried not to panic. She put her chin up. "I am paying tuition."

"Yeah, right. *How?*" Sienna said. "Living in a house like that?"

"I don't have to tell you anything." Throat tight, Mira pushed past her.

"Coach Wallace will be really interested to hear about this," Kendra called after her.

The rest of the day felt like a nightmare. Mira made herself so sick she wasn't even hungry for lunch. But she forced herself to go to the cafeteria and sneak some extra sandwiches. Her mom would be working late.

She couldn't focus on anything in class. She kept expecting to hear her name called to the principal's office.

At the end of the school day, she decided to do something she'd never done in her life. She skipped tennis practice.

It was a risk. She knew Coach Wallace would be furious. They had the match against Bremerton tomorrow. She just couldn't face him right now. She was afraid if she did, she'd throw up right at his feet.

She dragged herself home after school. She was sad that she was missing practice but relieved she didn't have to face Coach.

Later that night, after Sean was in bed and she was watching TV, Mira checked her phone. There was an e-mail.

Trembling, she opened it.

Hi Mira,

I saw you at school today, but you didn't come to practice. You also didn't e-mail me to let me know. If there's an emergency, I hope you let me know as soon as possible what's going on. If it's not an emergency, you know that skipping practice without telling me is unacceptable.

Being on the team means taking it seriously. That means

communicating with me. I expect you at the match bright

and early tomorrow.

-Coach Wallace

CHAPTER 9

ACE

The next morning, Mira was filled with dread as she collected her stuff for the match. Her mom and Sean were coming to watch for the first time. She'd told them a million times to be careful of what they said. It seemed especially useless to say this to Sean. He didn't understand why they needed to keep secrets. "Why does it have to be a secret where we live?" he asked.

"It just is," Mira said, impatient. "Just promise me you won't say anything."

73

"OK, OK, I promise," he said.

Mira loaded her stuff into her mom's car and got Sean settled in. Then her mom drove them to Bremerton Middle School.

"I'm proud of you," her mom said in Hindi, as they pulled into Bremerton's parking lot. She had a huge smile on her face. "My girl is an athlete and a scholar."

Mira managed a laugh. "Thanks, Mom. I'm glad you're coming."

"You know I'm proud of you no matter what," her mom said. "You're such a brave, smart girl."

"I love you, Mom."

Addie's parents had just parked too, and came to greet them. Mira was glad to see that Henry had come along too. Maybe he would keep Sean occupied.

Coach Wallace, of course, pulled Mira aside immediately. He asked what happened. She lied and said she must have eaten something bad and felt so sick she had to go right home. She apologized for not telling him. He looked suspicious, but he let it go.

She went to the locker room, depressed. The excitement she'd felt just a few minutes ago was draining away after all.

"Put it out of your mind, Mira," Addie told her. "Focus on the match."

Mira tried to feel excited for the match. She kept glancing at Kendra and Sienna. When they first came into the locker room, they were smirking and happy. But as they started warm-ups, Mira noticed Kendra looked angry. She was frowning and her face was scrunched up.

"What's wrong with her?" muttered Mira. "Why's she so mad?"

"*Stop obsessing, Mira*," Addie whispered, standing in front of her so she couldn't stare at Kendra anymore. "Focus on the game."

They spun their rackets to see who was up when. Mira was up last. She hated being up last, but she'd just have to deal with it.

Hilltop won most of the matches. Addie and her

partner, Courtney, won their match. Both Sienna and Kendra beat their opponents too.

Finally, it was Mira's turn. She was up against Laura Chen. Laura had an amazing first serve. Mira knew if she could survive it and keep Laura running, she should be OK.

Laura was ready. "Love serving love!" she shouted.

Her serve had a mean angle and drew Mira wide, so she had to hustle back to center court. After that, she got into a rhythm. Laura tried to surprise her with a drop shot. Mira lobbed it back with a forehand. Laura had a powerful top spin that drew Mira back away from the net. The first chance she got, she charged the net for a volley, Mira's strong suit. But hard as Mira played, by the end of the first set, Laura was winning 6–4.

Coach Wallace pulled her aside. "Good job. You're hanging with her. Focus on returning that first serve. Keep her moving."

So that's what she did. The top of the second set,

Mira returned Laura's serve. She could tell Laura was starting to get flustered. Mira was up 40–15, and then Laura double faulted. Mira had broken her serve. She won her own service game easily, putting her up 2–0 at the start of the second set. The next thing Mira knew, she'd won the whole set.

The third set was vicious. Laura had talked to her coach and seemed to have rallied. Mira served first and faulted. Her second serve, Laura returned with her famous drop shot. Mira was ready for it. She flew forward and lobbed it back to her backhand. She stayed close to the net and volleyed.

She prayed Laura wouldn't return it with another lob. That would mean Mira would have to run. Instead Laura tried to sneak it straight up the line, right to Mira's forehand. That was the perfect place for her to win the point with a tight angle volley.

After that, Mira sent Laura sprinting to the net as often as she could. Laura was so flustered she hit the ball long. Mira kept her moving, staying close to the net. She glanced at the score. She was up 5–4, and the game score was 40–15. If she won the next point, she'd win the match.

Laura knew it, too. She was breathing hard, bouncing on her toes. Mira hit the first serve long. She saw Laura move up a step, ready for her safe and slow second serve. That was when Mira made the decision to take a risk. She served her first serve again—fast and low to Laura's backhand. Laura wasn't ready for it. She swung late. And missed. Mira had aced her!

Applause rang out. Coach Wallace and her teammates went wild in the stands. Mira's mom and Sean cheered alongside Addie's family. Sean was even standing up and jumping up and down. So was Henry.

Mira stepped to the net to shake Laura's hand. Then she turned and threw her hands in the air.

She was elated as she stepped off the court. Her back, arms, and feet were sore. She didn't even care. She was just so happy.

Coach Wallace patted her on the back. He was beaming. "Awesome job, Mira."

Addie hugged her. For a second, it was like Mira didn't have a worry in the world. It was like she was just any other kid on the team. She didn't think about money or grades or mowing lawns or being exhausted. It was the best feeling on earth.

They headed back to the locker room for a shower and change.

"Coach was really happy with you," Addie whispered to her. "It doesn't look to me like you're about to get kicked off."

Mira forced herself to smile. She was so happy that she'd almost forgotten she was worried about getting kicked off. She didn't want to get her hopes up.

Once they were out in the school hallway, she pulled out her phone to check the time.

A new e-mail notification popped up on her screen.

She read the subject line. Mira couldn't believe her eyes.

"Addie!" She groped for Addie's hand. "Addie—it's for the scholarship!"

"Open it!" Addie squealed.

Mira sank down on a bench in the hall. Her legs were too shaky to stand up. She looked around to make sure no one was close by. She opened the e-mail and read:

Dear Miss Ravi,

We were very pleased to receive your application for our scholarship. We're delighted to inform you that you've been chosen as our deserving recipient this year. If you wish to accept the scholarship, we will need to reach out to your parent or guardian and your coach to verify information and to better understand your situation. We look forward to hearing from you. Congratulations!

Sincerely,

The Rick Morris Memorial Scholarship for Student Athletes Committee

Mira's entire body deflated. All her hopes for the scholarship went out the window.

For her to get the scholarship, they would need to talk to Coach Wallace. And then it would all be over. Her hopes of getting the scholarship would be finished. She wouldn't even be allowed to stay at the school.

Mira looked at Addie as her eyes filled up with tears.

And that's the exact moment Coach Wallace walked up to them.

CHAPTER 10

A BIT OF HELP

Coach Wallace sped up when he saw Mira was crying. He knelt down in front of her. "What's wrong? You did a great job out there!"

Addie patted her back. "It's not that, Coach." She hesitated, then said, "I think you should tell him, Mira."

Mira hiccupped and sniffled. She pulled herself together enough to glare at Addie. What was she thinking?

"I mean it." Addie sounded firmer than Mira had

ever heard her. "It's too stressful for you to keep it quiet."

"Keep what quiet?" asked Coach Wallace, his brow furrowed.

Just then, Kendra and Sienna came out of the locker room. They stopped when they saw that Mira was crying. Kendra smiled. She hadn't looked that happy the entire day, even after they'd won the match.

"What's wrong?" she asked. She tried to sound casual.

"Nothing," said Coach Wallace. "Head on home. Great match, girls."

Smirking, Kendra and Sienna walked out.

He turned to Mira, looking truly worried now. "I can't help you if you don't tell me what's going on."

Addie nudged her. Mira took another shaky breath. Then, it all spilled out. She told Coach Wallace where she really lived, out of district. And that she'd been lying.

"And the other stuff," Addie said quietly. "Tell him what's going on at home too."

Mira glared at her again. But she made herself take another breath. She told him about her mom and Sean and the scholarship. She told him she was sure she wouldn't get it now, since she'd lied.

As he listened, his expression changed. It went from coach-face to worried-face.

When she was done, he patted her on the shoulder.

"Mira," he said, "I'm glad you told me. Congratulations on the scholarship, first of all."

She held her breath. She was waiting for him to say *But you were dishonest, so you're off the team.*

Instead he said, "I'd like to help however I can. I wish I'd known some of this sooner. I understand why you felt like you couldn't tell anyone." Then he frowned. "Is worrying about all this why you skipped practice yesterday?"

"No, that's because of Kendra!" Addie burst out. Her face was red. She kept going. "Kendra and Sienna followed Mira home yesterday. Then they threatened to tell you where she really lives. They want Mira off the team."

Mira had never heard Addie so upset. Her mouth was set and her eyes were blazing.

Coach Wallace shook his head slowly. "I'm sorry that happened, Mira. Before the match today, Sienna did mention that you live out of district. But I wasn't aware of how she learned that information. We don't tolerate bullying at this school. I will be addressing their behavior."

"They *told* you?" Mira squeaked. She was confused. Why did he let her play, if he already knew she'd been lying?

Before Mira could ask, Addie fumed, "That's why Kendra was so mad today! She was hoping you'd kick her off the team once you found out."

Coach Wallace shook his head. "I'll have a talk with her, for sure. That's not how teammates treat each other."

Mira felt a flood of relief that Coach Wallace believed her about Kendra. But she was still holding her breath. Mira waited for him to tell her she was off the team for lying.

"I'm sorry I lied," she whispered.

"Listen, Mira. I didn't grow up with a lot either. I didn't go to a school like Hilltop. I know what it's like. I'm very happy to have you on this team and at this school. I know how much strength it takes for you to be here."

Mira couldn't believe what she was hearing. She dared to look at him now.

"I'm happy to talk to the scholarship committee. There are other scholarships available too," he said. "We might be able to get you an academic scholarship that will cover out-of-district tuition. Like I said, I'll help however I can."

She stared at him. How could it be that Coach Wallace knew the truth and was willing to help her anyway?

"Mira!" Addie bounced on the bench excitedly. "This means you'll get the scholarship!"

She still couldn't believe it. "So . . . I'm not off the team?"

"No, of course not," he said. "I'm very proud of you. Now more than ever."

Mira felt as if a million pounds lifted off her chest. She could breathe deeply for the first time since she came to Hilltop. Her mom would be so happy.

And then, even though she was excited for herself, she found herself thinking about what Mr. Meyers said about paying it forward. Maybe she would be a tennis pro someday. If she was, she knew she'd use her fame to help kids who needed it. Kids like her. The idea felt like a warm spark in her chest.

And even if she wasn't famous, there would be ways to help. Like Coach was doing now.

"*Thank you*, Coach," she said. She'd never meant "thank you" more in her life. "Seriously."

Addie hugged Mira. Just then, Mira's mom and

Sean came around the corner of the hall, followed by Addie's parents.

"There you are," Mira's mom called in Hindi, smiling.

Sean raced toward her. "You were awesome, Mira!"

She got up, beaming, and ran to tell them all the news.

ABOUT the AUTHOR

Salima Alikhan has been a freelance writer and illustrator for fourteen years. She lives in Austin, Texas, where she writes and illustrates children's books. Salima also teaches creative writing at St. Edward's University and English at Austin Community College. Her books and art can be found at www.salimaalikhan.net.

GLOSSARY

ace (AYSS)—in tennis, it's a legal serve that isn't touched by the receiver, winning the point

backhand (BAK-hand)—a shot when a tennis player swings the racket around their body with the back of the hand before the palm

drop shot (DROP-shot)—hitting the tennis ball so softly that it hits the ground right after clearing the net

forehand (FOR-hand)—a shot made when a player swings their racket across their body with the hand moving palm-first

eligible (EHL-ih-gih-buhl)—able to be chosen for something or receive something

let (LEHT)—if the ball hits the net but still makes it over the net, it's called a let and the serve can be redone

lob (LOB)—hitting the ball high and deep into the opponent's court

seed (SEED)—in tennis, a term used to categorize the players most likely to win

tuition (too-ISH-uhn)—the fee, cost, or payment for going to certain schools

volley (VAW-lee)—a shot in which the ball is struck before it bounces on the ground

DISCUSSION QUESTIONS

1. Mira has many stresses that prevent her from being able to focus on school. Talk about some of these stresses, and why they were so hard on her.

2. Mira's life experience is very different from the experiences of her tennis teammates. How are her experiences different? How do they affect how Mira sees the world?

3. Kendra bullies Mira throughout the story. Why do you think she was so focused on Mira? Do you think how Mira handled being bullied was right?

WRITING PROMPTS

1. Mira feels like an outsider and like no one at her school or on her tennis team can really understand her life. Write about a time you felt misunderstood.

2. Mira lies to her school about where she lives. She also takes food from the cafeteria. Do you think these actions are right, wrong, or somewhere in between, given Mira's circumstances? Write out your opinion.

3. Mira writes an essay about her life to apply for her scholarship. What do you think her essay said? Write your version of Mira's scholarship essay.

MORE ABOUT THE SPORT

The game of tennis comes from Great Britain. Wimbledon is the name of the oldest tennis tournament in the world. It started in 1877, and it's held in London, England, every year. It's also the only major tennis tournament still played on grass! Most courts these days are made of concrete or clay.

The first women to play Wimbledon had to wear full-length dresses and corsets. Eventually, they were allowed to wear more comfortable clothing.

Yellow tennis balls were first used at Wimbledon in 1986. Before that, tennis balls used in the tournament were white.